For my dad
– S. S.

For Lily, Holly, Harry, Jack,
Daisy, and Ben. Love Claire x
– C. P.

tiger tales
5 River Road, Suite 128, Wilton, CT 06897
Published in the United States 2022
Originally published in Great Britain 2022
by Little Tiger Press Ltd.
Text copyright © 2022 Suzy Senior
Illustrations copyright © 2022 Claire Powell
ISBN-13: 978-1-68010-276-5
ISBN-10: 1-68010-276-1
Printed in China
LTP/2800/4079/0821
10 9 8 7 6 5 4 3 2 1

www.tigertalesbooks.com

OCTOPANTS
AND THE MISSING PIRATE UNDERPANTS

by Suzy Senior

illustrated by
Claire Powell

tiger tales

Hello! Come in and welcome
to our world beneath the sea.

Meet Puffer Fish and Turtle, too,
and Octopants — that's me!

I once tried finding underpants
and didn't have much luck.
But someone called me "Octopants,"
and, well, the name just stuck!

But Puffer Fish wears underpants,
and usually, that's just fine.
But once, his favorite pirate pair
went missing from the line.

"Come on," I said to cheer him up.
"Let's go and track them down!"
So off we went, with tons of snacks,
and searched all over town.

We looked in
Lobster's Laundry . . .

and we checked in
Mermaid's Hair . . . .

We tried in Mussel's Fitness Club:
the underpants WEREN'T THERE!

"We're out of luck!" sobbed Puffer Fish.
"Ohh, what a pointless trek!"
"Hey, wait!" I said. "We can't give up.
Let's go and search the . . .

. . . WRECK."

"The shipwreck? YIKES!" yelled Puffer Fish.
"It's creepy!" Turtle cried.
"I hope your undies aren't in THERE!"

We bravely peered inside.

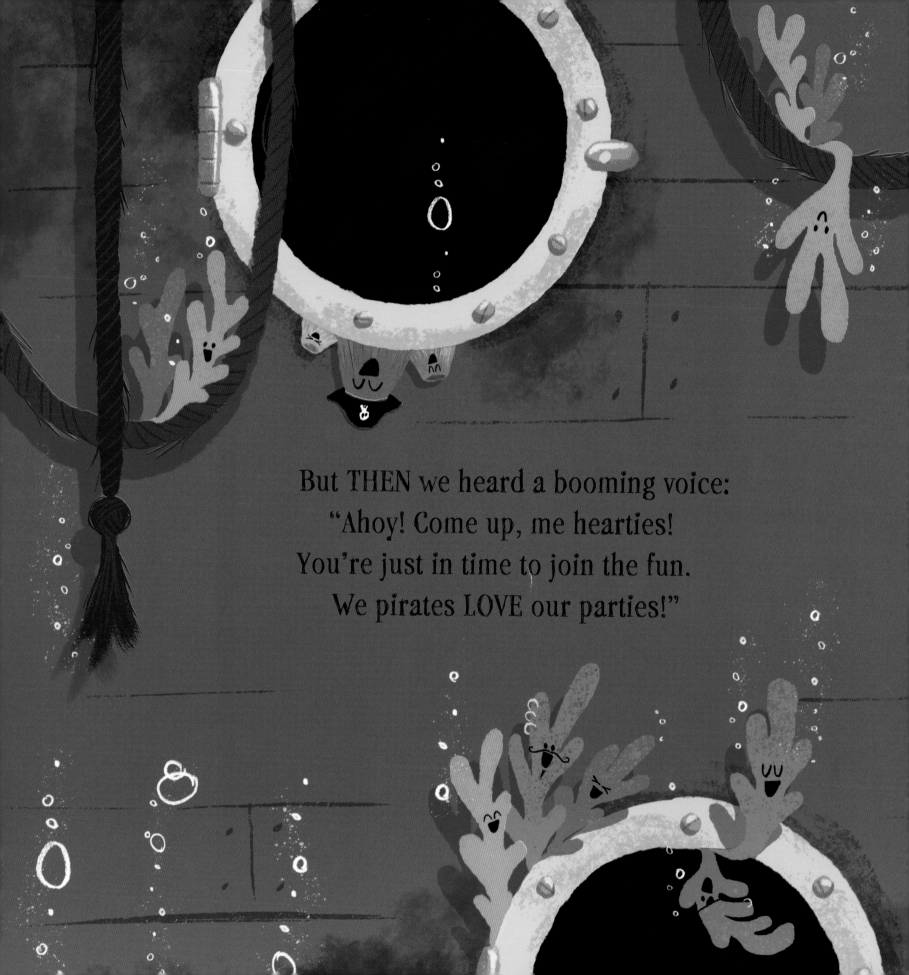

But THEN we heard a booming voice:
"Ahoy! Come up, me hearties!
You're just in time to join the fun.
We pirates LOVE our parties!"

And there they were, a pirate crew
in undies of all sizes:
pants with anchors, pants with bows,
and pants for cool disguises!

Rainbow pants
and disco pants . . .

and pants to make
you tougher.

Yes, UNDERWEAR was EVERYWHERE —
but NONE belonged to Puffer!

"Avast! You lost your underpants?
How sad!" the pirates cried.
"We'll come and help you search for them.
Now where would undies hide?"

Just then, a shadow crossed the deck.
It all went cold and dark.
We saw a flash of giant teeth . . .
and Turtle shouted . . .

. . . "SHARK!"

"She's after us!" yelled Puffer Fish.
"We have to get away!"

We raced past ropes and cannonballs,
but then the shark called, "HEY! . . .

I'd like to join your pirate crew.
I have a hat!" she said.

Then Puffer laughed.
"My UNDERPANTS . . .

...are sitting on your HEAD!"

The shark looked stunned. "Your underpants?
    I found them in the kelp!
Here, take them back."
    And Puffer smiled,
        "Hey, thanks for all your help!"

"Hooray for pirate pants!" we cheered.
    "Let's celebrate!" And SO . . . .

We joined the pirates back on board
to PARTY! YO, HO, HO!